Rainbow Love

Rainbow Love

by
Joan Walsh Anglund

DETERMINED PRODUCTIONS, INC.,

ISBN 0-915696-51-7
Library of Congress catalog card number 82-70028
Printed in Singapore
First Edition
Published by Determined Productions, Inc.
Box 2150, San Francisco CA 94126

For Dr. Gerald G. Jampolsky
and
the children
at the
Center for Attitudinal Healing
who have learned
to turn fear
into
Rainbows
of
Love.

Believe!
   ...and Rainbows appear.

Endure the storm,
   ...but remember
      the Rainbow!

Rainbows
are the
smiles of God.

Friends,
    like Rainbows,
        brighten our days.

Unless we lift our eyes,
we cannot see
the Rainbow.

Happiness consists
of turning Life's storm clouds
into Rainbows.

We each have a choice...
we can stay under a cloud,
or get busy,
and find our Rainbow.

A Rainbow is that glorious child
born of the sunlight
...and the showers.

Beyond the clouds,
    ...waits the Rainbow!

We must each paint
    our Rainbow from the
        colors we've been given.

We must always
remember to take
our Rainbows with us!

Through the dark days,
keep a Rainbow
…in your heart!

A Rainbow
is the bridge
to Heaven.

...Follow Your Rainbow...